Pink
Power

Pink
Power

Lorna Schultz Nicholson

James Lorimer & Company, Ltd., Publishers
Toronto

James Lorimer & Company Ltd. acknowledges the support of the Ontario Arts Council. We acknowledge the support of the Government of Canada through the Book Publishing Industry Development Program (BPIDP) for our publishing activities. We acknowledge the support of the Canada Council for the Arts for our publishing program. We acknowledge the assistance of the OMDC Book Fund, an initiative of Ontario Media Development Corporation.

Cover design: Kate Moore and Meghan Collins

Library and Archives Canada Cataloguing in Publication

Schultz Nicholson, Lorna

    Pink power : the first women's hockey world champions / Lorna Schultz Nicholson.
(Recordbooks)

ISBN 978-1-55028-989-3 (bound)
ISBN 978-1-55028-987-9 (pbk.)
    1. Hockey for women — Canada — Juvenile literature. 2. Women hockey players — Canada — Juvenile literature. 3. Hockey — Tournaments — Canada — Juvenile literature. I. Title. II. Series: Recordbooks (Toronto, Ont.)

GV848.6.W65S38 2007   j796.962'0820971   C2007-904397-6

James Lorimer & Company Ltd., Publishers
317 Adelaide Street West, Suite #1002
Toronto, ON
M5V 1P9
www.lorimer.ca

Distributed in the United States by:
Orca Book Publishers
P.O. Box 468
Custer, WA USA
98240-0468

Printed and bound in Canada

Contents

To the inspiring women of the 1990 Pink Power team, for paving the way for young girls who aspire to play for Team Canada.

Prologue

Would anyone want to watch women play hockey?

The International Olympic Committee (IOC) looked at each other. They had gathered to talk about a problem. The 1988 Olympic Winter Games had just passed, and people felt there were not enough women taking part. The president had an idea: women's hockey! Hockey was a team sport, so it would bring in lots of female athletes. But would it attract fans?

The IOC met with another group: the International Ice Hockey Federation (IIHF). They agreed it was an idea worth testing out. The IIHF would hold a women's world hockey championship. Canada was asked to host it. This was a huge risk, but they took it.

Some people had doubts. Women's hockey was different from men's hockey. Female players are not as strong. They don't shoot or hit with the same power. People loved to watch women figure skate … but play hockey?

1 Who Will Go?

The day dawned bright and cold in Sherwood Park, Alberta. Mail carrier Shirley Cameron went to work as usual. It was just like every other day until she checked her own mailbox.

She flipped through her letters. There were a couple of bills, a flyer — and something from Hockey Alberta. She ripped open the envelope and read:

You have been selected by the

Alberta Amateur Hockey Association
to attend the National Women's Team
Selection Camp.

Shirley had grown up shooting pucks
on outdoor rinks. She started playing
hockey back when girls wore figure skates.
They shoved newspaper under their pants
for shin pads. It was a long time before her
teams started getting indoor ice time.
When they finally did, they had to go on
at eleven o'clock at night. Shirley was now
37 years old, there had never been a world
championship in women hockey.

Shirley clenched the letter. Only six
women from Alberta would be trying out.
She was one of the six! She wanted to make
it so badly. She was getting on in age for an
athlete, and this could be her last hurrah.

She would have to train hard.

In Edmonton, Judy Diduck got the

same letter as Shirley. She was also a talented ringette player. If she made the team, she might have to play in *two* world championships in the same month. Judy folded the letter and smiled. For years she played road hockey with the boys. Her brother Gerald was now a defenceman for the New York Islanders. If he could play top hockey, so could she. She was going to the tryouts in January.

Susie Yuen came to hockey much later than most serious players. She grew up in Winnipeg playing sports with her brothers. She was never given a chance to play hockey. Instead, her parents put her in ringette when she was ten. Susie finally found her true sport in university. A friend suggested that she try out for the girls' hockey team. "Sure," said Susie. "What do I have to lose?"

At the first practice, Susie was embarrassed. She didn't have the proper hockey gear. (She was also just 4-foot-10-inches tall — quite small compared to most players.) The next day she went to Canadian Tire to get hockey pants and gloves. In time, she became a key player for the University of Manitoba's Women's Hockey Club.

A few years later, Susie entered a meeting room at the university. She had seen a notice on a bulletin board. It said there was going to be a meeting about a national women's hockey team. Manitoba would be sending just three players to the tryouts. Susie glanced around the room. Few women had shown up. Who would be chosen?

At the end of the meeting, the women who wanted to try out were asked to sign a sheet. Susie's was the third and last name on the list. She waited to see if anyone else was going to sign up. No one did. Would she get to go to the hockey camp just because no one else wanted to?

Diane Michaud pulled her hockey bag out of the trunk of the car. Her hands were freezing. It was getting very cold in Montreal. She quickly unlocked her apartment door and dropped her gear to the floor. As she blew on her hands to warm them up, the phone rang.

"Bonjour?"

That fall, Diane had moved to Montreal from Quebec City to play hockey for the Sherwood team. She was now one of the top players in Quebec. The voice on the phone was full of excitement. It said Diane had been hand-picked to try out at the National Women's Team Selection Camp.

Diane was pleased to find out she knew the other players from Quebec who were going to try out. France St-Louis was the best female player in the province. Another France — France Montour — was awesome too. Goalie Denise Caron could stop shots as well as any male player.

Diane hung up feeling thrilled but a little concerned. She hadn't gone to many tryouts. Usually, she was just chosen for a team. How would she perform under this new kind of pressure?

When Stacy Wilson got off the phone she was in shock. The New Brunswick Hockey Federation had just given her the good news. The physical education teacher couldn't believe it. A world championship was in the works! And she had been invited to the tryout camp!

Women's hockey was not as big on the east coast as it was in places like Toronto. Just six easterners were going to the tryouts. There would be three from New Brunswick, two from Newfoundland, and one from Prince Edward Island. Stacey felt honoured and nervous to be among them. As she returned to grading her students, she began to worry. How would she get time off from her classes if she made the team?

2 Ontario Tryouts

Ontario would select its players differently than the rest of the country. It had way more women playing hockey than any other province. Fran Rider, head of the Ontario Women's Hockey Division, decided to hold open tryouts.

In the Brampton arena, team members from the Brampton Candettes gathered around a bulletin board. Dawn McQuire pointed to a letter posted there. It explained that twelve Ontario players would go on to attend the "real" tryouts for the national team.

Dawn picked up her bag and checked the clock. It was midnight already. She had to get up at six for her job at Cobblestone Paving. Dawn had moved from Alberta for work, and now she juggled her job and playing hockey. At twenty-nine, she was not ready to quit the sport she loved so much. If she made the team, then what? Playing in a world championship was a chance of a lifetime. She'd have to ask for time off from work. Dawn shook her head. There was no point even thinking about that yet. She had to get through the Ontario tryouts first.

Angela James lived in Toronto. She worked for Seneca College in the Recreation Department. She was also one of the best players in Ontario. When her coach told her about the national team, she knew she would try out.

Word travelled and women talked. The best of the best were all set to try out, including Heather Ginzel, Margot Verlaan, Theresa Hutchinson, Brenda Richard, and goalie Cathy Phillips.

North York Aeros player Geraldine Heaney also wanted to try out. She had come to Canada from Ireland. But she still did not have her immigration papers or a Canadian passport. She worried that she would not be able to play on the team without them.

Sue Scherer lived in Kitchener, Ontario, where she was the general manager for her brother's car dealership. Her family also had a leasing company, of which she was the general manager. Sue was a softball player for the national team and her family was great about giving her time off. She knew her brother wouldn't mind if she missed work to go to the tryouts. She marked her calendar in red.

Vicky Sunohara showed up to hockey practice at Northeastern University (NEU) in Boston. She was very excited. Both Vicky and her teammate Laura Schuler were from Ontario, attending NEU on hockey scholarships. Vicky had been playing hockey since her father taught her the game at age two. At five, he put her on a boys' team. Laura plunked her bag down beside Vicky. At eighteen, Laura was the youngest on the team. Her teammates in the dressing room were all talking about the world championship.

THE NEXT GENERATION

"I was only three years old in 1990. To me the women who played in 1990 are pioneers and I'm so thankful to them for what they did for women's hockey in Canada."

— *Meghan Agosta, 2006 Olympic gold medallist and Team Canada player since 2004.*

Vicky and Laura had received phone calls from Dave McMaster, the University of Toronto's women's hockey coach. He asked them to fly home for Canadian Thanksgiving to attend the Ontario camp.

Dave had been asked by the Canadian Amateur Hockey Association (CAHA) to coach the Canadian team. He was the only women's coach in Canada with enough experience to coach a national team. His University of Toronto Lady Blues were at the top of their game. They had won the Ontario women's university championship in eight of the past ten years. Both Vicky and Laura had played on teams with some of his players.

Although most of the talent in Ontario came from the south, there were a few good players from other parts of the province. Ottawa girl Kim Ratushny was at Cornell University in New York State. The school had given her a hockey scholarship. When she heard about the tryouts, she ran over to her younger brother's dorm and rapped on his door. Dan was also on a hockey scholarship at Cornell. He hoped to play on the Canadian National Junior Team at Christmas. All her life, Kim's hockey had taken a back seat to Dan's. He always had better ice time, and could try out for national teams. He also got better gear, and his teams always had more money. Now it could be her turn to wear Canada's red-and-white uniform.

On the day of the tryouts, hockey players of all shapes and sizes showed up. They filled every dressing room in the Mississauga arena. They were all hoping to be picked for the main selection camp.

Goalie Cathy Phillips, who played for the Hamilton Golden Hawks, had only a short drive to Mississauga. Breakfast hadn't gone down well. The bagel seemed to sit like a log in her stomach. Was her sickness just nerves? She hadn't been feeling well for a few weeks. Today of all days, she had woken up with a splitting headache.

When Cathy got to the arena, she scanned the competition. She counted eight goalies strapping on pads. Most were pretty young. She wondered how many were in the other room.

Usually her dressing room was noisy: players sang and talked. This morning the buzz was a low drone. Everyone discussed the championship. What would it be like to play in a world event? Cathy tried not to listen.

Cathy stepped onto the ice in her goalie equipment. She saw twenty other goalies there. Her head still pounded — but she didn't let it stop her. The Golden Hawks goalie stopped shot after shot. She did what she had to do to get noticed. Her vision was off, though.

After the first hour, Cathy had a three-hour break. She got something to drink and tried to eat. She still felt sick. Then she was back on with the forwards.

Fifteen minutes into the next session, she knew she had to stop. She skated to the bench where Fran was taking notes on the players.

"Fran," she said. "I don't feel well."

"What's the matter?"

"Migraine. I have to get off the ice."

Fran patted Cathy on the shoulder. "Please come back on Monday. There will be an exhibition game. You have to play in the game to make the cut."

Cathy nodded.

The weekend was packed with tryouts for the Ontario women. Then, it came down to the final day and a big exhibition game. When the game was over, Fran and the other decision-makers had a list of sixteen players. They just couldn't cut it down to twelve.

Dave, the team coach, decided all sixteen would attend the main camp.

The list was posted in the arena lobby.

3 Coaches' Corner

Snow fell in huge flakes from a grey sky on January 13, 1990. Forty-six nervous players arrived at the Meadowvale Four Rinks Complex. They came to Mississauga from 10 of Canada's 12 provinces and territories. The camp roster had six goaltenders, 16 defence, and 24 forwards. They were competing for just twenty spots.

Cathy was feeling a little better than she had at the Ontario tryouts. But she still wasn't one hundred percent. She had a hard time looking to the left. Sometimes she even saw two pucks. Cathy kept this all to herself. She wanted to play for Team Canada no matter what.

Many players had problems they pushed aside. Stacy didn't let herself think about her students. Vicky and Laura had left their schoolwork behind. Other players tried not to worry about the work they were missing. To make the team, each player had to live, breathe, and sleep hockey.

Inside the rink, Dave sat in the stands. He had a clipboard resting on his knees. He chewed on the end of his pencil as he watched the players skate. "What do you think?" he asked his assistant coaches. Their names were Rick Polutnik and Lucie Valois.

Rick had never coached women's hockey before. However, he'd run many clinics for female players in Alberta. He knew the technical side of the game. Rick knew the Alberta players well, but he wouldn't play favourites. He was on the lookout for talent.

The CAHA wanted a woman with hockey smarts on the staff. Lucie knew the game very well from coaching in Quebec. She also spoke French, like the players from her province.

All the players had been given either a red or a white jersey. "I like red number 23," said Rick, tapping his pad of paper. "She's fast and handles the puck well."

"*Oui*. That's France St-Louis," replied Lucie. "She is very good."

"I also like that little player. She's small but fast."

"I don't know," Dave said. "They're allowing body checking. She's not even five feet tall." He put a tick by her name anyway. "I think she's someone to watch in the intersquad game on Sunday. See how she handles the big girls."

One by one, the coaches reviewed every player on the ice. They each had a check sheet. That's where they wrote notes about skating, passing, shooting, and hockey sense. Hockey sense is like common sense — on the ice! It means knowing where to be at the right time.

When Dave, Rick, and Lucie left that first day, there was no media waiting for them. A press release had been sent across the country announcing the tryout camp. No reporters came.

The coaches spent five days taking notes in the cold arena. By the end, they had ranked every player. They tried to put a list together that went from best player to worst. It had been easy to pick the top and bottom five. The rest were tougher to decide upon. Each coach had a different opinion. They started with a group of 14 definite players. Then they made another list of 10 who were "being looked at."

Dave opened the notebook. He knew that some of the players "being looked at" were actually the best. They just hadn't done well at the camp. "I still think we can pick the full team at this tryout," he said.

Rick shook his head. "I don't think we can or should." He believed that every player had to have had a good camp. He didn't want to rely on how they played in the past.

"What do we tell the ones who we're still looking at?" Dave asked.

"That we will be watching how they play when they get back with their club teams. And that we'll decide between now and the beginning of March," said Rick. "We can't do another camp. This is our only option."

Dave nodded. Rick had a point.

This last day of camp was the most important. The red team was facing off against the white team. It gave the coaches a chance to see the players in action. After the final game the coaches brought the players together. The women were told that they would each have a meeting with the coaches. The coaches would tell them whether they had made the team or not. Some would find out they were still being looked at. The meetings would be held first thing in the morning.

The player looked at each other nervously. That night, many of them tossed and turned. Who had made the team, they wondered? Who would be going straight home?

4 Welcome to Team Canada

Vicky woke up and looked at her clock. Five-thirty a.m. Her meeting was scheduled for 6:10. She got up, quickly showered, and pulled on her sweats.

Vicky took the elevator to the coaches' floor. Laura, her friend from Northeastern University, was already there. She was sitting cross-legged on the carpet outside the meeting room. Vicky sat down beside her. "What time is your meeting?"

"6:20."

"You're early."

"I couldn't sleep."

The door opened. Vicky and Laura glanced up at the player coming out. Her face was red and wet with tears. Vicky sucked in a deep breath. What if she didn't make it? Her stomach knotted and her throat felt dry.

Dave stood at the door. "Vicky, you're next."

Vicky slowly entered the room. Lucie and Rick greeted her with smiles. "Vicky," Dave said, sticking out his hand. "Welcome to Team Canada."

"Are you kidding?" Vicky's entire body shook. She closed her eyes and tried to compose herself. When she opened her eyes, she grinned from ear to ear. Then Vicky put her hand in Dave's. He smiled and shook it.

Vicky listened carefully to everything the coaches told her. The tournament was scheduled for March 19 to 25 in Ottawa. The team would get together on March 12. It was important for her to arrive in top shape. With her information package in hand, Vicky left the room.

As soon as Vicky saw Laura, she jumped up and down. "I made it!" she yelled.

"That's fabulous!" Laura said. "I knew you would, though."

Vicky blew out a rush of air. "Good luck." She patted Laura on the back, as Dave called her in.

Canadian Women's Team dressed in pink track suits in Ottawa, Ontario.

Laura's stomach rolled like a big wave. She tried to read the faces of the coaches. What were they going to tell her?

"Welcome to Team Canada, Laura," said Dave.

Laura screamed and jumped up and down, just like Vicky had. She hugged Dave. Then she pulled back and looked at the other coaches. Their happy faces made her scream and hug Dave again.

Dave started laughing. "Hey," he said, wiggling out of her grasp. "You're hugging me so hard my tie clip is digging into me."

Laura put her hand over her mouth and giggled. On her way out, she turned and hugged Dave one last time.

Vicky was waiting for Laura. "I made it! I made it!" Laura yelled. They hugged and screamed. The Northeastern teammates would be playing together for Canada.

Kim's alarm went off at 6:30. Although she knew her brother wouldn't be awake yet, she reached for the phone. Dan would understand. He had played for the Canadian National Junior Team at Christmas. His team had won the gold medal in Helsinki, Finland. He told Kim it was the best experience of his life. There was nothing like wearing the red-and-white uniform for your country!

Dan answered after three rings. "Hello." His voice had a groggy, scratchy sound.

"Hey, it's me. Sorry to wake you up. I'm waiting to go to my meeting."

"Good luck," Dan said.

"Thanks."

"Phone me as soon as you find out."

"I will." She looked at the clock. "I gotta go, okay?"

The coaches picked just 14 players. Nine were from Ontario: Kim, Vicky, Laura, Cathy, Sue, Theresa, Brenda, Margot, and Dawn. France St-Louis and Diane from Quebec made the team. So did Judy and Shirley from Alberta. Susie, the lone player from Winnipeg, rounded out the roster.

The new teammates were given white track suits with pink lettering down the sleeves. Pink ball caps topped off the outfits. The women thought the colours were an odd choice. Still, they put them on and posed for a photo. Soon enough, they would step on the ice, proudly wearing red and white.

The names of the 14 players were made public later that day. Kim, Sue, and France St-Louis went to the announcement at the Hot Stove Lounge in Toronto. Then they posed for a media picture by one of the goal nets at Maple Leaf Gardens. The photo shoot made them realize that their dreams were coming true.

Later, Kim boarded a plane, heading back to Cornell University. She looked out the small window. The sky was a beautiful turquoise and full of white, puffy clouds. She had trained so hard and the work had paid off. Now she was a member of Team Canada. The press release about the new team sat in her lap. Every so often, she looked down and read her name. She kept thinking, "I am on the national team. I am a member of Team Canada."

Some players weren't having such a nice evening. Ten had been told they were "being looked at." They knew they were good enough. Why hadn't the coaches picked the full team?

IN IT FOR THE LONG HAUL

Vicky Sunohara is the only player from the 1990 team who is still playing on Canada's National Team. Since 1990 she has played in three Olympic Winter Games (1998, 2002, 2006) and eight IIHF World Championships.

After meeting with the coaches, Angela and Heather packed their bags. They were upset. Both were top players in the Ontario Women's Hockey League. It didn't seem fair. As they left the hotel, their hearts were as heavy as their suitcases.

Denise and France Montour went back to Quebec. Denise had already made up her mind. The coaches had only named one goalie. There was no way she was going to let this chance slip away. She would show them that she should be the other goalie.

Fun-loving France was quiet on the way home. She didn't laugh or crack jokes like she usually did. She would do that only after she made the team.

5 Behind the Scenes

Angela and Heather got ready to prove themselves. They were a little angry and very determined.

Angela knew the coaches had their eye on her. There was no fooling around when she took to the ice with her regular team. She gritted her teeth and played tough hockey.

Less than a week after the first 14 players were named, Angela got a phone call. She had made the team.

Heather got her call a few days later.

That left just four spots. Geraldine ranked high on the list. There was one problem: she was a landed immigrant. This made the organizers at the CAHA office in Ottawa very nervous.

Murray Costello was the president of the CAHA in 1990. He got one of the vice-presidents, Pat Reid, to oversee the Canadian team. Kathy Joy was the team manager. She worked as the manager of Female Hockey and Recreational Hockey. Frank Libra, a CAHA volunteer, was to be chairman of the tournament. Pat, Kathy, and Frank would work together.

Right away, Kathy worked on getting Geraldine a passport. The coaches wanted her on the team as soon as possible.

Kathy worked on the tournament details. Things did not go well. There was no help from the CAHA. It seemed more interested in other events. Murray told

Kathy to drop all her other CAHA work and focus on the tournament.

Kathy wrote letters and made phone calls, working closely with Frank. She sent out dozens of press releases. There was some interest from the media, but not enough to sell tickets for the games. Kathy didn't know how else spread the word. Time was pushing onward. The tournament was in less than two months.

Murray was sitting back in his chair,

This is the jersey that the Canadian women wore. The maple leafs were pink.

thinking about this problem, when Pat knocked on his door. Pat's job was to find sponsors. Sponsors help pay for things like jerseys and gear. Pat was creative and he always had new ideas. However, Murray wasn't ready for Pat's latest. In fact, he was speechless.

Put the women in pink jerseys and white pants?

Murray stared at Pat. What was he thinking? After a few seconds of silence, Murray said, "Absolutely not."

Pat spent fifteen minutes trying to change his mind. Murray was firm: Canadian hockey players wore red and white. No Canadian team would wear pink jerseys.

The days slipped by. The coaches finally figured out the last three players on the roster of twenty.

When Stacy got her call, she was overjoyed. But the teacher knew it would be tough to get more time off school. Her principal hadn't been thrilled when she left for the tryout camp in January. Kathy — now working twelve hours a day — offered to help Stacy with her school board. Stacy didn't want to lose her job.

Denise from Quebec was chosen as the other goalie and France Montour as a winger.

The game schedule was organized and sent to the media. Canada's first game would be on Monday, March 19 against Sweden. Again, the media showed almost no interest. Murray was getting anxious.

Murray met with Bob Nicholson, vice-president of Domestic Hockey for the CAHA. They chatted about the team roster and the coaches. Then Pat joined the meeting, plunking his big briefcase on the table.

Once again, Pat wanted to talk to Murray about the pink jerseys. Bob glanced at Murray and shook his head.

Pat didn't give up. He explained that a company called Tackla was a new sponsor. They would do a pink jacket and rugby-type jersey. The jerseys would be beautiful and classy. The clincher: the jerseys might draw in the media.

Murray sighed. Pat was wearing him down. This was the third time he'd brought it up with Murray. And they had to do something to get the media's attention. Without it, the tournament would be a huge flop.

Murray asked Pat to show him what the jersey looked like. Bob frowned as Pat snapped open his briefcase. "I don't agree with this," he said. "I think it's a crazy idea."

Murray knew Bob liked to see the Canadian teams in red and white. Murray did too. But maybe Pat had something here. Ticket sales weren't exactly booming. Maybe his ideas would help fill the stands.

"Okay," said Murray. "Why don't we take a look first before we make any decisions?"

"We don't need to look at anything!" Bob stood up. "We have a design. A traditional Canadian hockey design! Canadians wear red and white."

"I agree with you," said Murray, "but we might have to do something to get the seats in the arena filled."

"We don't have to fill the seats this way."

"Come on, Bob, let's just give this some thought."

"I don't want to be any part of this."

Bob stormed out of Murray's office.

Murray sighed and ran his fingers through his hair. Pat ignored the fight and laid the drawings on the table. The sweater had a huge maple leaf on the side. The leaves were bordered with a steel-grey colour. The pants were white with the same side trim as the maple leaf design.

The socks had a white trim to match.

Pat used many different words to describe the main colour. He called it washed-out red, strawberry red, and blush red. Murray knew the jersey was pink. He kept staring at the drawings. How would the country react to their national team wearing pink?

How would the players react when they heard the news?

6 Pink Stinks!

Shirley received another letter from CAHA. What could it be? She had already received her travel plans in a previous letter. It had contained the game schedule too. It explained how to prepare and what to expect. It had been a long and detailed letter. She ripped this second letter open.

Shirley flipped to the last page and saw that the letter was from Pat. She read about the team gear. She read about the team jerseys. Then she got to the part where it described the team colours. The letter said: "The colour scheme is a washed out red — almost pink colour."

She stopped reading. Were they really going to make them wear pink jerseys? White-and-pink track suits were one thing, but jerseys?

When Shirley got home, she picked up the phone and called Judy. "Did you get that last letter from Pat Reid?" she asked.

"I did," replied Judy. She paused. "What do you make of it?"

"I don't know."

"Do you think the jerseys are . . . going to be pink?"

"I think that's what washed-out red means."

Judy started laughing. "White pants will be disgusting!" She paused again. Then she said, "But what can we do?"

"Not a thing. I still want to play no matter what."

"Me too."

Before Sue opened her letter, she got a call from Kathy. The women knew each other well from playing on the national softball team. Kathy said, "Sue, you'll love this. The jerseys are blush red."

Susie Yuen and Stacy Wilson with big smiles posing for a shot.

"You mean pink," replied Sue.

"Exactly."

"You could put us in grey and I'd be happy," said Sue. And she meant every word. Who cared about jersey colour? She was playing for Canada.

Murray met with Kathy, Pat, and Frank to discuss the upcoming press conference. They were going to unveil the pink jerseys, pink socks, and white pants. Pat planned to have a mock jersey there to show the media. He couldn't wait to see their reaction.

Murray still wasn't convinced that the media would show up. He went along with Pat anyway. Murray admired Pat's enthusiasm and positive energy.

Press releases announcing the pink jersey went out to radio and television stations as well as newspapers across the country. At the last minute, Kathy realized that Judy was in Ottawa for the World

Ringette Championship. Kathy asked her to attend the press conference and model the jersey.

This was even better, thought Pat. A live model. He was excited.

When Murray walked into the press room, he was amazed. It was jammed with reporters, cameras, and microphones.

Frank stepped up to the mic and thanked everyone for coming. Then he introduced Pat. Pat presented Judy, who appeared before the crowd wearing the pink jersey.

The cameras started clicking. The room buzzed with reporters asking questions.

"Why pink?"

"Isn't this a disgrace to women's hockey?"

"Why would you do this to the women?"

"Are you trying to stereotype the women?"

The questions kept coming.

The next morning a *Toronto Star*

headline declared: "Pink Stinks." The jersey had made the front page of Canadian newspapers. This started a flurry of other media. The jerseys were discussed on radio talk shows across Canada.

The players also talked about the jerseys, but only amongst themselves. Most of them agreed that the white pants were also a bit much. They thought that the organizers of this event had not got it right.

But the women on the team refused to let any of this bother them. No one raised a big fuss. No one went to the media to say how silly the jerseys were. No one talked openly about the uniform. They wanted to step onto the ice in an official IIHF World Hockey Championship. They could win a gold medal for Canada. They could make history. That was the most important thing.

7 March 1990

March arrived too soon for some of the players, but not soon enough for others. Stacy's principal had still not given her the okay to leave her classroom. And Kathy was still waiting for Geraldine's immigration papers.

The players were scheduled to arrive on March 12.

It was only days before that Stacy's principal said she could have the time off. Then Geraldine's papers and passport came through. Kathy breathed a sigh of relief. It was time for the games to begin.

Players arrived on flights from all over Canada and the USA. They had big hockey bags and one suitcase each.

The first night, all the players checked in at the hotel. They wore their white sweatsuits and pink hats. The hot-pink hats became a team joke. They were big and

HOCKEY HEROES

"The entire 1990 Women's World Championship Team are my heroes and the players that I grew up emulating. Without the dedication of this generation of players the Olympic dreams of so many athletes would not have come true. The players of today owe everything to this group of passionate women."

— *Cassie Campbell, 2002 and 2006 Olympic gold medallist and Team Canada player from 1994 to 2006.*

didn't sit really well on their heads. The women put them on anyway.

Upon their arrival, all the teammates were given bright pink warm-up suits. These were the suits they were to wear to the arena on game days.

The first practice was on March 13. In the coaches' room, Rick shook his head as he pulled out his track suit. It was hot pink. He could handle the pink jacket; he wasn't sure about the pink sweatpants. Rick looked at Dave. "Do we really have to wear these?"

Dave held up his hands. "It's our uniform."

"Okay," said Rick. "Here goes."

The pink track suit looked a lot better on Lucie than it did on Dave and Rick. When the players saw the coaches step onto the ice wearing pink, they hid their snickers behind their gloves.

The team had just five practices to get

ready before their first game. They would play against Sweden on March 19. Rick loved working with the women. They were more eager to learn than the men he'd coached. When he blew the whistle, they skated as hard as they could to the bench. They listened to every word he said. They asked questions if they didn't understand something.

Rick, Dave, and Lucie met to discuss their strategy for the game against Sweden. The coaches knew that no team could be taken lightly.

The tournament schedule was a round robin. The eight teams playing had been divided into two pools of four. Canada's pool included Sweden, Germany, and Japan. Rounding off the other pool were Norway, Finland, Switzerland, and the USA. The Americans were the Canadians' big rivals. After the round robin, the top two teams in each pool would play each other in a semi-final game. The winners of the semi-finals would go on to the playoff for the gold-medal game. The losers of the semi-finals would play in the bronze-medal match.

Was the Canadian team ready to play? Could they make it to the gold-medal game?

On March 19, the women arrived at Lansdowne Park. They wore their white-and-pink team track suits and pink hats. Their matching pink jackets had Team Canada written on the front and the back.

The arena was empty: the game didn't start for another two hours. As they filed into their dressing room, their footsteps seemed to echo off the arena walls.

The players hung their pink jerseys on hooks. They were each given two jerseys, two sets of socks, and one pair of pants.

Sue couldn't help but look at the big "C" on her jersey. She had been honoured when her teammates voted for her to be captain. She planned to take her role seriously.

The women didn't talk much as they put on their hockey gear. No one complained about their uniforms. They wanted to prove that Canadian women could play hockey whether they wore red or pink.

In the dressing room, the team listened closely to Coach Dave. He told them to play their game. He told them to forecheck and backcheck and skate hard. He called out the lines.

The team named the lines just for fun. France St-Louis, France Montour, and Sue were "the French connection line." Sue at centre connected the two French wingers.

Heather, Stacy, and Shirley were "the coast-to-coast line." Shirley was the west coast player, Heather was from mid-Canada, and Stacy was the east coast player.

Vicky, Susie, and Laura were "the kid

line." They were the youngest players on the team. Sometimes they were called "the ponytail line" too.

Margot, Angela, and Kim were "the Ontario line."

When the team stepped onto the ice, the fans screamed. It was hard for the players not to look at the crowd. Most of the team had never played in front of this many people before. The arena wasn't sold out, but it was full.

Throughout the stands was a spattering of pink.

8 Unexpected Injury

When the ref dropped the puck, the Canadian players skated hard. The Swedish women, dressed in yellow and blue, didn't have a chance. In their flashy pink jerseys, Team Canada controlled most of the play.

The first goal was scored by Angela after one minute and twenty-nine seconds. The fans went nuts. Her teammates rushed over to Angela and hugged her.

Sweden made a brief comeback in the

first period. Three minutes later, they tied the game up. But the Canadian women scored four more goals before the siren sounded to end the first period. Shirley, France Montour, Dawn, and Heather each scored one goal.

The Canadians filed into the dressing room.

Coach Dave told them to keep playing their game and to shoot the puck. He told them to rack up the score.

Good advice. By the end of the game, the score was 15 to 1. The Canadian team really had shot the puck! Angela popped in four of the goals. Sue sunk two to the back of the net. Shirley picked up her second on a slap shot. The rest of the goals had been spread out with France St-Louis, Vicky, Brenda, and Stacy.

There had been few shots against the Canadian net. Cathy found it tough to play in goal when there weren't many shots. So far her health had been not great, but okay. She had gone to the doctor after the Ontario camp and they had ruled out multiple sclerosis. The goalie would have more tests in May.

The next morning, newspapers across Canada wrote articles about the game. In some, the articles were small and difficult to spot. But in others the women made the front page. They were now nicknamed the Pink Power team. They tried to ignore the press but they couldn't. Women's hockey had never made big headlines before.

Behind the scenes, Murray and the CAHA office staff were pleasantly surprised with the first crowd. But the biggest surprise was when a producer from The Sports Network (TSN) called to say they wanted to televise the Canadian games. They liked how the players dug for the puck and skated hard. They liked the team's tough, gritty style along the boards. Well-known sportscasters Howie Meeker and Michael Landsbury would host the event.

Murray sat in his office tapping his pencil. What had started as a little snowflake was now a snowball.

Women's hockey would come to living rooms across Canada. Who would have thought that could happen?

As team manager, Kathy knew that she needed to keep the snowball growing. Before the next practice, she went to just about every store in Ottawa to buy pink tape. It took her hours to find enough, but she did. Then she went early to the rink with Michelle Patry, who was the third goalie on the team. They taped all the sticks. When the women arrived for practice, they were shocked but pleased. They were even more pleased when they heard about the television coverage.

Canada was to play Germany on Wednesday, March 21 at 7:30 p.m. The

Canadians couldn't wait to step onto the ice in their pink jerseys.

The women arrived at the Earl Armstrong arena two hours before their game against Germany. They were nervous and the dressing room was quiet. When the coaches announced that the ice was ready, the players marched out. Television camera lights hit their faces to capture the moment. The lights were shocking. Was this for real? The Canadian team was greeted by an even bigger crowd for this game. The arena was smaller but it was packed. The pink spots in the stands seemed to be getting bigger. Sue sucked in a deep breath. By the stunned look in many of the players' eyes, she knew she had to hold the team together. The captain could not let her team get distracted.

Once again, the Canadians dominated. Three minutes and twenty-three seconds into the first period, Heather popped the puck into the net. One minute later, Laura snuck another puck past the German goalie. As the youngest player on the team, Laura was now known as Baby Schu.

By the end of the first period, the Canadians were up 5 to 0. The other three goals were scored by France Montour, Stacy, and Vicky.

The goals kept coming for the Canadians in the second period. Two-and-a-half minutes in, Angela scored her first goal of the game. Then a minute later Baby Schu scored her second goal. Just one-and-a-half minutes later, Heather scored her second goal. The Canadian team was on fire — and there were no signs of them letting up. Twelve minutes into the second period the score was 10 to 0 for the Canadians. Baby Schu picked up another goal to give her a hat trick and Susie got her name on the score sheet with a goal.

The game was definitely going Canada's

way. That is, until deep into the second period.

France St-Louis battled hard along the boards. She knew how to play tough. She was Canada's power player. The Quebecer had the puck on her stick when, suddenly, she felt something on her throat. Her head snapped back. She fell to the ice.

The ref blew the whistle. France didn't get up. The Canadian team trainer flew onto the ice. She raced over to France and got down on one knee. France couldn't talk. She writhed in pain.

The trainer helped France up and everyone in the arena clapped. Players from both teams tapped their sticks on the ice. When they returned to the bench, the trainer said, "She needs to go to a hospital."

Kathy got France in her car and sped off. The closest hospital was fifteen minutes away. As Kathy drove she kept glancing at France. The injured hockey player could hardly breathe. She hoped she would be okay. And Kathy had another worry: what if France couldn't play in the semi-finals? What if she missed the gold-medal game?

Cellphones were not common in 1990. Kathy had no way of knowing the score of the game. She looked for a television set in the hospital waiting room. There wasn't one. While France was with the doctors, Kathy paced. It wasn't the game she was worried about — Canada would surely win — it was France.

France was admitted to the hospital and ordered not to talk to anyone. She had taken a nasty high stick to the throat. They wrapped her throat and put a tube down it to help her breathe.

Kathy was standing at the foot of France's bed when a nurse came in. "I just heard Canada won 17 to 0," she announced.

"All right," Kathy punched the air with her fists.

France could not scream or yell. But she did manage to squeak out the words, "Will I be able to play our next game?"

"The doctor will have to decide that," said the nurse. "Remember, you're not supposed to talk."

Tears spring to France's eyes. She had to play in the next game.

When France was settled in, Kathy headed back to the hotel. She found out that Angela had lit up the third period. She scored three goals to make her total four goals in the game. Susie and France Montour each put in another goal to give them two goals for the game. Shirley scored one goal. And Baby Schu scored one more goal to round her total to four.

All the players were anxious to hear about France. They circled Kathy.

"She has to spend the night in the

hospital," said Kathy. "And she can't talk to anyone."

"That will be tough," said France Montour. She loved to be the life of the

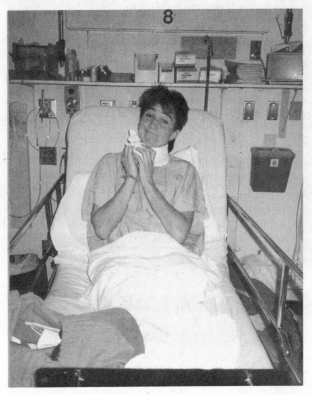

France St-Louis in the hospital after being hit in the throat.

party. The woman from Quebec couldn't imagine not being able to talk.

As captain, Sue spoke for the team. "Do you think she'll play against Japan?"

Kathy shrugged. "I have no idea. We'll have to wait until tomorrow."

Everyone crossed their fingers. They could probably do without France in the game against Japan. But they needed her back for the semi-final.

9 Final Round-Robin Game

France had to watch the next game on her little hospital television. The Canadian women took to the ice at the Barbara Ann Scott arena. The final game in their round-robin series was against Japan. She wanted to be there so badly. No one had visited France. She almost felt as if the team had abandoned her.

Her teammates had all wanted to visit France in the hospital. The doctors felt it would be better if they didn't, because she wasn't supposed to talk. They all missed her.

Even without France in the lineup, the Japanese team was no match for Canada. The Canadians won their third round-robin game 18 to 0. Once again the goals were divided: eleven players shared the scoring. Both Angela and Heather picked up hat tricks. Vicky, France Montour, and Shirley picked up two apiece. And Geraldine, Stacy, Margot, Dawn, Susie, and Kim scored one each.

The Canadians filed to the dressing room with a 3 to 0 record in the round robin. They wondered who they would play in the semi-final. And they wondered if France would be back to play. The semi-final was scheduled for March 24. So far in the B Pool the United States and Finland were tied. Each team had won two games. They played off in their last round-robin game at 7:30 p.m. at Lansdowne Park. The Canadians would play the loser of that game.

Canada had a day off in between games. The team still wasn't allowed to visit France. She would have to stay one more night in the hospital. If she was let out on Friday, she might be able to play on Saturday in the semi-final game.

The women gathered that night for dinner. Dave, Rick, and Lucie didn't want them to watch the USA versus Finland game. They would have to hear the score after the game was over.

To take their minds off things, Dawn and Brenda decided to go to the gift store for Peek Freans cookies. They had taken all the cookies when they were served for dessert that night. In the gift store, the cookies came in packages of four. They bought every package! Dawn and Brenda decided that the cookies were power. They would eat them before the games.

In a nail-biter, the USA beat Finland by one goal. The score was 5 to 4. Suddenly

1990 TEAM CANADA TOP SCORERS

Player	G	A	PTS
Angela James	11	2	13
Heather Ginzel	7	5	12
Susie Yuen	5	7	12
Shirley Cameron	5	6	11
Stacy Wilson	3	8	11

reality set in. Brenda and Dawn knew they needed more than cookie power to beat Finland on Saturday. The treats had been a good distraction but that was it. Although the Canadians had dominated in their round-robin games, their easy games were now over.

It was hard for the Canadian to enjoy their day off because of all the hype. The team had a morning practice and then had spare time. No matter where they went they were recognized. Fans loved their pink warm-up suits. Total strangers approached the players to wish them good luck. This had never happened to any of them before. Usually, no one knew anything about women's hockey.

Even the coaches felt the hype. After the team got off the ice, Rick decided to go to Sparks Avenue in Ottawa. He walked down the cobblestone street in his pink jacket. Every few steps, he was stopped by people wishing him luck. Good luck signs were plastered across the city.

The City of Ottawa and local businesses supported the Women's Hockey Championships.

The best luck of all came later that day: France was released from the hospital.

10 A Close Semi-Final

On Saturday, March 24, the team met for breakfast. Everyone ate quietly. The game wasn't until 6:00 p.m. They were playing at the Lansdowne Park arena: the big rink. After breakfast they had a light skate. Then they had lunch. The day seemed to drag.

They all hung out together. With markers they doodled on t-shirts for inspiration. They drew a stick figure of a woman with a medal around her neck. On top they wrote, "Golden Child."

Judy took the marker and went up to Baby Schu. "I'm going to give you something to play for," she said. She drew a medal around Baby Schu's neck.

Dawn and Brenda were back at their cookie game. They bought all of the gift store's Peek Freans cookies again.

All afternoon, the team waited to hear the news about the USA versus Sweden semi-finals. They were playing in the afternoon at Lansdowne arena. Finally, as the Canadians were getting ready to head to the rink, the news trickled through the hotel rooms. The USA had beat Sweden 10 to 3 to make it to the gold-medal game.

This totally pumped the Pink Power team. They wanted to play the USA on Sunday — and no one else.

The Canadians boarded their bus. As they were the home team, each player carried her white jersey. So far in the tournament, they had always been the away team. That mean they wore pink jerseys. Their white jerseys were the same, except they were white and the maple leaves were pink.

Dressed in white, they stepped onto the ice. The fans roared. There were so many people at the game! The arena was at least three-quarters full. To the players it looked and felt like a sold-out game. There were pink banners, pink signs, and pink t-shirts.

Players gathered on the ice after the game to receive MVP awards.

The players' stomachs were full of butterflies.

Nerves felt different in this game. The stakes were much higher. Losing today meant they didn't play in the gold-medal game. The players knew how much support they had from the city of Ottawa and the CAHA. Now they understood the entire nation was behind them.

They knew they were expected to win.

The women gathered around the bench for their cheer and Coach Dave's pep talk. The crowd was cheering. The players had to lean close to hear. This was another televised game, so they would have to take breaks for the commercials. By now, the players had learned how a televised game worked. The puck had to drop at exactly the right minute to broadcast the game on television.

The Canadian starting lineup was the French connection line. On defence were

Brenda and Geraldine. Denise was in goal.

The five players lined up at centre ice. Nervous, they fidgeted while waiting for the cameras to signal the start of the game. The puck dropped when the red lights of the cameras went on.

The pace was faster and more furious than ever before. After just forty-five seconds, France St-Louis headed to the bench, waving her stick. She needed a line change. France Montour and Sue were not far behind her. On the bench Sue could hardly breathe, her heart was pounding so much. "We have to keep our shifts short," she said panting.

"I agree," said France Montour. "My legs were screaming."

The next line came off after a short shift too.

Less than two minutes into the game, on a pass from Vicky, Diane ripped the puck past the Finnish goalie.

The fans screamed. The players jumped up and down on their skates.

"We can do this," yelled Margot down the bench.

The play went up and down the ice for the next six minutes. At the halfway mark in the first period, Finland managed to nip one past Denise. The game was back to square one. The score was 1 to 1.

After Finland's goal, the coast-to-coast line lined up at centre ice for the faceoff. The ref dropped the puck and in sixteen seconds, Stacy made a great pass to Heather who popped the puck in the net. Stacy and Shirley hugged Heather. Then they skated over to Denise and patted her on the back. The tie had lasted less than a shift.

The score remained 2 to 1 for Canada until the last minute of play in the first period. With just forty-two seconds left, Vicky accepted a great pass from Geraldine on the point. The puck sailed into the net. The score was 3 to 1 for Canada when the buzzer went off.

In the dressing room, the players listened to Coach Dave. He told them to keep hustling, keep skating, and keep playing hard along the boards. Theresa rocked back and forth as she listened. When it was time to head back to the ice, she was focused and determined. Still, she didn't think they had the game in the bag. As defence, she didn't want anyone to get by her.

Four minutes into the second period France Montour picked up a pass from Sue. She popped the puck in the net to make the score 4 to 1.

But the Finns were not going to roll over and give up. They scored three minutes later and then six minutes after that. The score was now 4 to 3 for the Canadians. There were seven minutes left in the period.

Anything could happen in a 4 to 3 game and the Canadians knew it. One bad bounce and the game could be tied again. Canada fought hard along the boards but the Finns fought back. Both teams took penalties.

With just four minutes left, Finland took a penalty for charging. Canada went on the power play. Twenty-nine seconds into the power play, the coast-to-coast line scored again. Shirley passed to Stacy who gave it to Heather. Heather fired a low shot past the goalie. The fans loved the action and cheered so loud that the Canadians couldn't hear. The players rushed to the bench. They had a two-goal lead.

Less than a minute later the Canadians scored again. France St-Louis sunk it past the Finland goalie. The Canadian team went wild. They were all so glad to have France back in the lineup. Canada went to the dressing room after the second period with a 6 to 3 lead.

This game was far from over though.

In the third period, Finland battled hard

The three French-Canadian players holding the cup.
From left to right, France St-Louis, Denise Caron
(goalie), France Montour.

to come back. Canada kept taking penalties. They took four penalties in the first four minutes.

On a power play, only four minutes into the third period, Finland scored. The Canadians were frustrated. They kept trying to score but couldn't.

Then Finland scored with six minutes left. The score was now 6 to 5. The Canadian players became tense and kept looking at the clock. They had to hold on to their lead. If only they could score.

"No penalties," yelled Dave down the bench. "We can't afford for them to be on a power play."

The intensity of the game kept up right until the last moment. Finland pulled their goalie to put out six players. They shot puck after puck at Denise, but she stopped the shots. The Canadians won the game 6 to 5.

The Canadians raced from the bench to

congratulate Denise. They had made it to the gold–medal game!

They would play the USA on Sunday, March 25 at 3:00 p.m. The game was less than twenty-four hours away.

11 Going for the Gold

Sunday, March 25 is a day the Pink Power team will never forget. They woke up full of energy but very nervous. Again, the game was being televised. They knew that all across Canada, people were watching. The tournament was a hit.

That morning Dawn woke up one year older. It was her birthday: she was thirty years old. On the way down to breakfast, Stacy presented her with a birthday card and a pink Frisbee. Dawn was touched that her friend had remembered. This team meant so much to her. They had bonded in a way that was very special.

At breakfast, the team sang "Happy Birthday" to her. Dawn looked around at her teammates and friends and wanted to cry for joy. She decided to save her tears for after the game. Dawn wanted one present to celebrate her thirtieth birthday — a gold medal.

The coaches talked to the team while they were eating breakfast. The women were told that the game was soldout. Tickets sales had skyrocketed. All over Ottawa, people were trying to get tickets for the big game. The city had jumped on the Pink Power bandwagon.

The team was excited to have so many fans behind them. But they had to stay focused. The women would have to ignore the cheering and yelling and play hockey.

The players tried to listen to their

coaching staff. Some sat super still, almost like statues. Some tapped their fingers on their thighs. Some rocked back and forth in an effort to squelch their nervousness.

The team boarded the bus two-and-a-half hours before game time. They were the home team today so they carried their white jerseys. After loading all the gear and jerseys into the bus, they sat in their favourite seats. Everyone was quiet. All the teasing and fun had stopped.

Baby Schu and Vicky knew how good the USA team was. The head coach for the team, Don MacLeod, was their coach at Northeastern University. The USA goalie, Kelly Dyer, was their university team goalie. She was big, strong, and hard to beat.

When they got to the arena, they unloaded their gear. In a solemn line they walked to their dressing room. They taped their sticks and got ready to play.

Baby Schu was halfway dressed when she suddenly realized that she didn't have her jersey. Panic swept through the dressing room. What was she going to do?

Kathy spoke up. "I'll go back to the hotel," she said.

Baby Schu handed Kathy her hotel key.

Kathy ran to her car. She would take Bank Street. What she saw there stunned her. The image is still cemented in her mind: the entire street was a crowd of pink!

The sidewalks were jammed with people. Mothers held hands with their little girls wearing pink t-shirts. Many had faces painted pink. Some people carried pink pom-poms. Some waved pink flags. Some wore pink fake fur hats. There were old people and young people, but what Kathy noticed most was the little girls. They clearly couldn't wait to watch their heroes play hockey.

Kathy was lucky to be going against the traffic. Cars inched along on the other side, honking their horns. She drove as fast as she could to the hotel. Luckily, traffic had thinned on the way back.

In the Canadian dressing room, the coaches gave Baby Schu the spare goalie's jersey to wear for warm-up. She put it on and it hung to her knees. She kept waiting, hoping, to see Kathy come through the door.

When everyone was dressed and ready, Rick, Dave, and Lucie talked to the Canadian team. The pre-game talk was short and sweet. The women knew they had to play their own game. "We have a lot of talent in this room." Dave looked each individual player in the eyes. "Play simple Canadian hockey," he said.

The room hushed for a moment. Then the women broke out into cheers.

Dave held up his hand to quiet

everyone. "Don't get overwhelmed by the crowd."

Everyone sucked in a deep breath. They'd never played in a game like this before. Adrenalin ran through their blood.

Down the hall, the American coach was also pumping up his team. He had a different method. He read a letter to his team from President George Bush Senior. When the letter had come to his hotel room, he was stunned. It wasn't every day a team got a vote of confidence from the president! Women's hockey had caught on in a big way.

"The American people will be rooting for another Miracle on Ice," he read to his team. The American team could hardly believe that the White House had sent them a letter.

They left the dressing room ready to play hockey.

Cathy, the starting goaltender, led the

Canadian women out of their dressing
room. Although Cathy's health was still an
issue for her, nothing would stop her from
playing the game of her life. She held her
head high.

As soon as the Canadian women started
walking along the black runners to the ice
surface, they could hear the crowd. Energy
seemed to pulse through the concrete
walls. The Canadian players marched
forward. Baby Schu still wore the back-up
goalie's jersey.

Fans hung over the walls to get a
glimpse of the stars as they emerged from
the underbelly of the arena. Cameras
flashed. Television lights blinded them.

Baby Schu's parents watched the team
come out, but they couldn't see their
daughter's number. Was she not playing?

The entire arena erupted with screams
when Pink Power stepped onto the ice.
The stands were a sea of pink. The

Canadian women were overwhelmed. They stared and stared at the crowds.

The official total of 8,784 was the largest ever to watch a women's hockey game.

The noise was so loud in the arena that the coaches had a hard time talking to the players. Kathy arrived seconds before the game was to begin. She threw Laura her jersey. Baby Schu quickly put it on and breathed a sigh of relief. She was ready to play hockey.

The teams lined up at centre ice. Coach Dave put out the French connection line. Brenda and Geraldine were on defence.

The red television camera light went off and the ref dropped the puck. The adrenalin was so high for both teams that they took off flying.

The pace was fast, the play tough. Bodies crashed against one another trying to get the puck. The boards rattled, the glass shook. The Canadians seemed unsettled and nervous. Just two minutes and twenty-five seconds into the first period, the USA scored.

Canada headed to the bench for a line change.

Sue yelled down the bench, "There's lots of game left."

Dave told everyone to calm down. Rick walked behind the back of the bench, patting shoulders to get them to relax.

"We can do this," said Margot to Angela as they waited for their turn to go out. "We can win."

"Of course we can," said Angela. She was determined to win this game. Angela never backed down in any competition.

Both teams battled for the puck and played hard hockey along the boards. The Canadians pushed and the Americans pushed back.

With four minutes and forty seconds

left in the first period, the USA team popped another goal by Cathy. She sucked in a deep breath. Her teammates skated over to her, telling her it was okay. They patted her shoulders and gently hit her pads with their sticks.

Dave put out the French connection line. Just eighteen seconds later, France St-Louis accepted a pass from Geraldine on defence and skated toward the net. At the edge of the crease, she fired off her shot. It sailed past the USA goalie to put the Canadians on the scoreboard.

"Go Canada go! Go Canada go! Go Canada go!" The noise from the crowd was deafening.

With less than two minutes in the first period, Judy broke out. All alone, she skated toward the USA goalie. The fans screamed. Judy ignored them. In a skilled move, she tucked the puck into the net on the far side.

The Canadian bench went crazy. The fans yelled. Pink swayed back and forth in the stands.

The Canadians had come back from a two-goal disadvantage to tie the game.

The buzzer went and the period was over.

Both teams filed to their dressing rooms to let the Zamboni clean the ice.

12 Digging In

The Zamboni driver was dressed in a pink flamingo suit. He had also decorated his Zamboni with pink plastic flamingos. The machine drove around and around the ice. During the break, young girls bought pink t-shirts in the arena lobby.

In the USA dressing room, the American women read the letter from the president again. They wanted to take it to the bench.

In the Canadian dressing room, Coach

Dave told his team to settle and play simple hockey.

Dave's speech must have worked. In the second period, the Canadians stepped onto the ice a different team. They had calmed down. The fans were now just a blur of pink. The team had a job to do and they were going to do it.

Team Canada shot and shot at the USA goalie. They dominated the play. But they couldn't get the puck in the net.

Just when it seemed like nothing was going in, France Montour saw an open puck. She dove on the ice, pushing her stick toward the puck. Sue touched the puck and it glided over to France St-Louis. She saw defence Geraldine along the boards and passed it to her.

With the puck on her stick, Geraldine rushed forward. She headed straight to the net. She deked by one USA defence. Then came a huge body check. Geraldine knew she was going to tumble, but she kept her eyes on the puck. As she flew through the air, she took a shot. The puck sailed high to the roof of the net. Geraldine crashed hard and slammed into the boards.

She didn't care. Her goal was in! The crowd was on its feet. Canada now had a one-goal lead.

The Zamboni driver in the final game dressed in a pink flamingo costume.

Geraldine's goal became a top ten TSN goal for the year 1990. TSN played it over and over for the rest of the year. Geraldine had put women in the mix with the men.

Howie Meeker called her the Bobby Orr of women's hockey. TSN sportscasters had already compared Angela to Mark Messier because she could body check. They also said little Susie was fast like Yvan Cournoyer from the Montreal Canadiens.

France Montour skated over to Geraldine, screaming, "That was amazing."

Geraldine replied, "It's just a goal. We need another one."

Geraldine didn't want to rest on one goal. She wanted the Canadians to get another to clinch the game.

However, no more goals were scored in the second period. But the Canadians out-shot the USA team 10 to 3.

When the Canadians took to the ice again for the third period, their fans could taste the gold medal. They screamed as the players stepped onto the ice.

Ten minutes and fourteen seconds into the third period, Susie slipped the puck by a goalie — who was almost twice her size! The fans loved little Susie. When she scored they let her know it by their loud cheers.

With just thirty seconds to play in the third, France St-Louis fired the puck into an empty net. She picked up her second goal of the game. Although she had spent two nights in a hospital bed, she was a star that day. She picked up four points in that final game, with two goals and two assists. She still couldn't talk very well, but she definitely could play hockey.

The Canadians beat the USA with a 5 to 2 victory.

They stood on their blue line and listened to the Canadian national anthem. Many of the players cried tears of joy. With pride, they sang the words they knew by

An excited Susie Yuen holds the plate in victory after the gold medal game.

heart. They couldn't stop smiling — or crying. They stared upwards at the red-and-white Canadian flag being raised. Never before had it looked so beautiful. When the anthem ended they suddenly came out of their silence. The champions screamed and hugged one another.

"Happy Birthday, Dawn," yelled Stacy over the noise. Dawn grinned. Their win was the best birthday present ever.

As captain, Sue accepted the gold plate for her team. Every player wanted to touch it, to feel it. They took turns skating around, holding it up. The women waved to their pink-coloured fans as they gave the team a standing ovation.

Afterwards, their fans waited for them. They wanted their pink-taped sticks. They thrust programs and pens at players, in the hopes of getting an autograph. Smiling, the Pink Power women signed autographs for fans who gushed over them as if they were

NHL hockey heroes.

The whole team gave willingly to their fans. They felt tremendous pride knowing they had encouraged young women to defy the odds.

They had made history.

FINAL STANDINGS IN THE 1990 WOMEN'S WORLD HOCKEY CHAMPIONSHIP

1)   Canada
2)   USA
3)   Finland
4)   Sweden
5)   Switzerland
6)   Norway
7)   Germany
8)   Japan

Epilogue

The first IIHF women's world championship was such a success that Finland hosted a second one in 1992. This time, the Canadians wore blue pants and fuchsia-coloured jerseys. Throughout the tournament, talks continued about adding women's hockey in the Olympic Games. On July 21, 1992, the IOC voted to add women's ice hockey as a winter Olympic event. It would be a full medal sport starting in 2002. Then, on November 17, further meetings were held in

2007 reunion in Winnipeg, Manitoba, of the 1990 Women's Team.

Japan. That country would host the 1998 Olympics. It was announced that women's hockey would be an official medal sport at the 1998 Winter Olympics.

When the Canadian women's hockey team stepped onto the ice at the 1998 Olympic Winter Games, they were finally wearing the traditional red-and-white jerseys.

In 2007, at the Women's World Ice Hockey Championship in Winnipeg, Manitoba, the 1990 Pink Power team reunited to celebrate their championship.

Seventeen members of the original team came. They were honoured on the ice during the first and second periods. The 2007 Canadian team wore the retro pink jerseys for their first game in the tournament. They wore these pink jerseys with pride, knowing that the 1990 team had paved the way for them to play Olympic hockey. In every game after that one, however, the 2007 team wore their true team colours: black pants and the traditional red-and-white jersey.

STRIKING GOLD

Starting with their first competition in 1990, the Canadian Women's National Hockey Team has won nine of ten IIHF World Championships (1990, 1992, 1994, 1997, 2000, 2001, 2003, 2004, 2007). They took silver in 2005, losing to the USA in a shootout.

So far the team has racked up 11 gold medals, including their wins in the 2002 and 2006 Olympics.

Where They Are Today

Shirley Cameron – Shirley, the oldest member of the 1990 team, lives in Edmonton, Alberta. She is a letter carrier for Canada Post and has been for many years. She has two dogs, Katie and Maggie.

Denise Caron – Denise lives in St-Eustache, Quebec. She has worked for JAYMAR Canada for twenty-seven years as a production advisor.

Judy Diduck – Judy lives in Edmonton, Alberta. She is the assistant coach of the University of Alberta Pandas. Judy also has a promotional product company called "Just Stuff." She played ten years with the national team.

Heather Ginzel – Heather lives in Elora, Ontario. She is a high school teacher and guidance counsellor. She recently finished a four-year Healing program in Florida, and she has opened a Healing practice. Heather is a musician and plays in the band Big Love.

Geraldine Heaney – Geraldine is a part-time women's hockey coach at the University of Waterloo. She is also a full-time mother to her daughter Shannon. She played thirteen years on the national team. Her famous goal is still played on sports highlights. She is now a Canadian citizen.

Theresa Hutchinson – Theresa lives in Bethany, Ontario. She works with the Durham Regional Police Service as a detective. She has two children, Ben and Mackenzie, and she helps coach their hockey teams. She also refs a ladies' league in Port Perry.

Angela James – Angela lives in Richmond Hill, Ontario. She has worked at Seneca College as the manager of the Recreation Centre for twenty-two years. Angela has twins, a boy named Michael and a girl named Toni. The twins have an older brother, Christian.

Dawn McQuire – Dawn lives in Calgary, Alberta. She works as an operations assistant for Weyerhauser, a wood product company. She played two years with the Canadian national team. Every time she eats Peek Freans cookies she thinks of Brenda Richard.

Diane Michaud – Diane lives in Zurich, Switzerland. She is a hockey ref in the men's first and second leagues in Europe. She also refs the women's hockey playoffs in Switzerland. She has learned to speak German.

France Montour – France lives in St. Albert, Alberta. She is a processor operator at the plastic manufacturer AT, which is in Edmonton, Alberta. She played in the world championship in Finland in 1992. She is still the life of the party.

Margot Paige (Verlaan) – Margot is the head coach of the women's hockey team at Niagara University in Niagara Falls, New York. She lives in Stony Creek, Ontario. She has rescued and kept three cats: Tyler, Taz, and Huck. She cares deeply about animal rights. She is married to Don.

Cathy Phillips – The headache that Cathy had at the tryout was because of a brain tumour. She underwent surgery just after the tournament was over. Doctors removed some of the tumour, but they couldn't get it all. Cathy is fine now, although she does have memory and balance problems.

Kim Ratushny – Kim lives in Ottawa, Ontario, with her husband, Kent, and two children, Ethan and Emma. She graduated from Cornell University and went on to law school. She is taking time off from practising law to be a mom. She played one year with the national team.

Brenda Richard – Brenda passed away suddenly at the age of twenty-seven. She had been promoting women's hockey for the Ontario Women's Hockey Association in northern Ontario. Within a day of becoming ill, she died. She was three months pregnant at the time. Brenda left behind a husband and young child.

Sue Scherer – Sue lives in Ottawa, Ontario. She quit working for the family businesses and decided to devote her life to sport. She is a senior program officer with Major Games and Hosting for Sport Canada. Sue has two girls, Kaitlyn and Lauren.

Laura Schuler – Laura still lives in Boston, Massachusetts. She is the head coach of the Northeastern University's women's ice hockey team, the school she graduated from. She was a member of the 1998 Canadian Olympic team. Laura is definitely grown up, but she is still Baby Schu to her 1990 teammates.

France St-Louis – France is a phys. ed. teacher at CEGEP in Vieux-Montreal, Quebec. She also has her own hockey school. France retired from the Canadian team at the age of forty. She now knows her teammates didn't abandon her.

Vicky Sunohara – Vicky is still playing for the Canadian women's hockey team. She has won two Olympic gold medals. One is from the Salt Lake City Olympics in 2002 and one is from the Turino Olympics in 2006. She is hoping to play for Canada in the 2010 Olympics in Vancouver.

Stacy Wilson – Stacy lives in New Brunswick, where she is still a phys. ed. teacher. Obviously taking the time off to play hockey in 1990 didn't ruin her career. She went on to play for seven more years. Stacy was the captain of the gold-medal-winning team at the 1997 World Championship in Kitchener, Ontario.

Susie Yuen – Susie lives in Winnipeg, Manitoba, where she works at Peking Chinese Food, her family's restaurant. She is also enrolled at the University of Manitoba in the Department of Science.

Although the restaurant would miss her, Susie is thinking of going into radiology.

Dave McMaster – Dave made many important contributions to women's hockey. He was a pioneer and a special friend to many female players. Dave passed away in February 2003 of a heart attack. He was 62 years old.

Rick Polutnik – Rick lives in Red Deer, Alberta with his wife, Donna. They have two boys, Ross and David. After sixteen years with Hockey Alberta, Dave now has his own Sports Management Company. It's called TeamWorks Canada Inc.

Glossary

CAHA: Canadian Amateur Hockey Association. The CAHA was the governing body of hockey in Canada but the name of this organization was first changed to Canadian Hockey Association (CHA), and then to Hockey Canada. The name had to change when they allowed professional hockey players to play on their national teams.

Domestic Hockey: This is the hockey that takes place in Canada. All minor hockey is considered domestic hockey.

Final Game: The game that takes place between the two top teams in a tournament.

Hockey Canada: This is the current name for the governing body of hockey in Canada, from grassroots domestic hockey to international hockey.

IIHF: International Ice Hockey Federation. The IIHF was founded in 1908 and it governs, develops, and promotes ice and in-line hockey for both men and women in the world.

IIHF World Hockey Championship: Any IIHF hockey tournament has to fall under governance of the International Ice Hockey Federation.

IOC: International Olympic Committee. This committee was founded on June 23rd, 1894, to revive the Olympic Games that used to take place in Greece a long time ago. Now it is an international committee that supervises the summer and winter Olympic Games.

NHL: National Hockey League. This is the league where the best hockey players in the world want to play. All games take place in North America.

Olympic Games: The Olympic Games feature athletes from all over the world and they help to promote the Olympic spirit of peace. There are summer Games and winter Games.

Pre-Game Talk: The pep talk coaches give before a team takes to the ice for a big game.

Press Release: The letter that is sent to television and radio stations and newspapers with all the information regarding an upcoming event.

Round Robin Tournament: A tournament where each team plays all the teams that are in their pool.

Selection Process: The methods that coaches and organizers use to pick players for a team.

Semi-Final Game: When four teams are left in a tournament, two games will be played so all four teams get to play. These are the semi-final games. The winners advance to the finals to compete for gold and silver and the losers play in what is called the Bronze medal match. One team will finish the tournament without a medal.

Tryout: This is when athletes have to compete against each other to make a team.

Glossary

TSN: The Sports Network. Canada's national sports television station that features non-stop sports coverage.

Zamboni: This is the machine that cleans the ice at the arenas. It was invented by Frank Zamboni in the early 1940s. Frank Zamboni lived in Southern California and he had an idea about a machine that would help clean his own rink. Now the Zamboni machine that is used on rinks all over the world is named after him.

Acknowledgements

I found out that writing a Recordbooks volume requires help from a lot of people. First, I would like to thank my editor, Hadley Dyer. She always pushes me to get the best story possible and has this crazy instinct that always makes my books better. I would like to thank Hockey Canada for supplying me with photos and original game sheets. Julie Healy, Director of Women's Hockey at HC, deserves special thanks as she answered many of my questions and helped me get in contact with the players from the Pink Power team. Kathy Joy supplied me with her personal photos and stories. Rick Polutnik shared his personal 1990 team binder with me. Murray Costello answered my many phone calls. Other people who deserve thanks include Danielle Sauvigeau, Meghan Agosta, Cassie Campbell, Fran

Ryder. But most of all I have to thank all the women from the Pink Power team who so graciously answered e-mails and met with me when I was in Winnipeg. You are an amazing group of women, and because of your energy, I was able to piece together a story that was so worth telling.

About the Author

LORNA SCHULTZ NICHOLSON is a full-time writer in Calgary, where she lives with her husband, senior hockey official Bob Nicholson, and three children. She is the author of several popular books in the Sports Stories series including *Roughing*, which was shortlisted for the Golden Eagle Children's Choice Book Award.

Photo Credits

We gratefully acknowledge the following sources for permission to reproduce the images within this book.

Hockey Canada: p 51, p 87, p. 106, p 110, back cover top, back cover centre, back cover bottom, front cover top

Kathy Joy: p 35, p 43, p 71, p 77, p 81, p. 103